FRENCH FRIGHTS

James stared out of the window. Some year-eights were playing football on the sports field.

In the staff car park, a delivery lorry was dropping off great vats of oil and huge sacks of frozen chips at the kitchens.

There's Mrs Cooper gossiping with the driver. Bet she tries to get him inside for a cup of tea, James thought. *There's Ms Legg, jogging round the field, and there's a knight in armour, holding some hag's hand –* WHAT?!

'Zac, I need to show you something . . . Look!' James pointed out of the window and the boys saw the two ghosts sitting under a tree.

Zac was moving from foot to foot. His eyes were wide.

'This knight, he haunts L'Ecole de St Martin! He is a terror! He must have – how you say? – *followed* us here from Poubelle!' He shuddered. 'He won't be alone

**St Sebastian's School in Grimesford
is the pits. No, really – it is.**

Every year, the high school sinks a bit further into
the boggy plague pit beneath it and, every year, the
ghosts of the plague victims buried underneath it
become a bit more cranky.

Egged on by their spooky ringleader, Edith Codd,
they decide to get their own back – and they're
willing to play dirty. *Really* dirty.

They kick up a stink by causing as much mischief
as in inhumanly possible so as to get St Sebastian's
closed down once and for all.

But what they haven't reckoned on is year-seven
new boy, James Simpson and his friends Alexander
and Lenny.

The question is, are the gang up to the challenge
of laying St Sebastian's paranormal problem to rest,
or will their school remain forever frightful?

There's only one way to find out . . .

www.too-ghoul.com

FRENCH FRIGHTS

B. STRANGE

EGMONT

Special thanks to:

Lynn Huggins-Cooper, St John's Walworth Church of England Primary School and Belmont Primary School

EGMONT
We bring stories to life

Published in Great Britain 2007
by Egmont UK Limited
239 Kensington High Street, London W8 6SA

Text & illustrations © 2007 Egmont UK Ltd
Text by Lynn Huggins-Cooper
Illustrations by Pulsar Studios (Beehive Illustration)

ISBN 978 1 4052 3240 1

1 3 5 7 9 10 8 6 4 2

A CIP catalogue record for this title is available
from the British Library

Typeset by Avon DataSet Ltd, Bidford on Avon, Warwickshire
Printed and bound in Great Britain by the CPI Group

School versus...

Year-seven new boy
and chief spook-hunter

James Simpson

Headmaster's son
and official brainiac

Alexander Tick

Strong as an ox,
gentle as an
unusually tall lamb

Lenny Maxwell

. . . Ghoul!

Loud-mouthed ringleader of the plague-pit ghosts

Edith Codd

Young ghost and a secret wannabe St Sebastian's pupil

William Scroggins

Bone idle ex-leech merchant with a taste for all things gross

Ambrose Harbottle

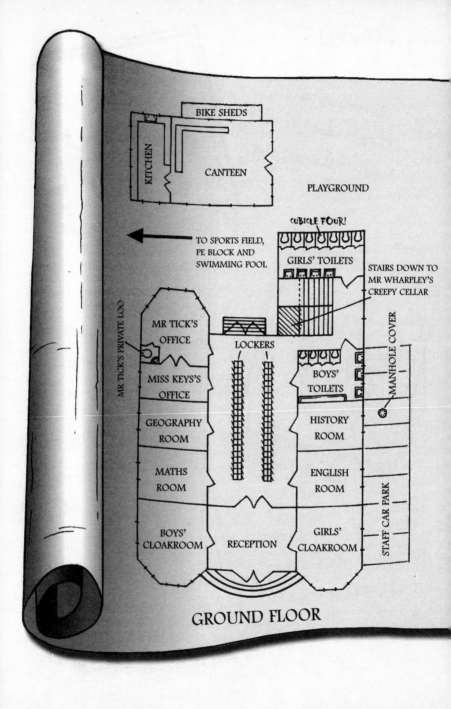

BIKE SHEDS

KITCHEN

CANTEEN

PLAYGROUND

CUBICLE FOUR!

TO SPORTS FIELD,
PE BLOCK AND
SWIMMING POOL

GIRLS' TOILETS

STAIRS DOWN TO
MR WHARPLEY'S
CREEPY CELLAR

MR TICK'S PRIVATE LOO

MR TICK'S
OFFICE

LOCKERS

MANHOLE COVER

MISS KEYS'S
OFFICE

BOYS'
TOILETS

GEOGRAPHY
ROOM

HISTORY
ROOM

MATHS
ROOM

ENGLISH
ROOM

STAFF CAR PARK

BOYS'
CLOAKROOM

RECEPTION

GIRLS'
CLOAKROOM

GROUND FLOOR

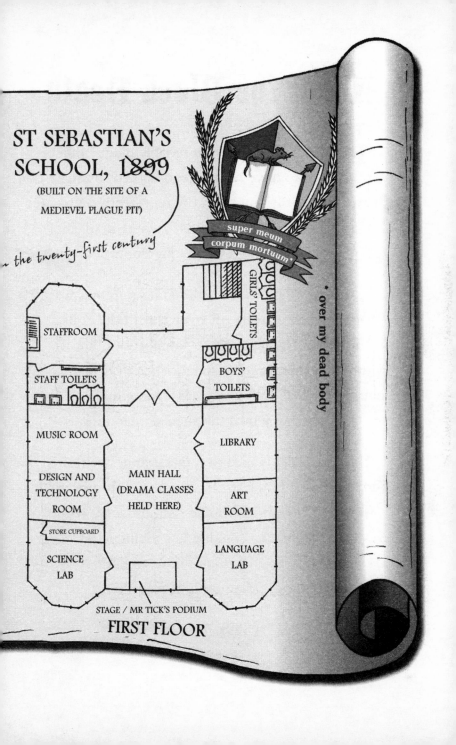

About the Black Death

The Black Death was a terrible plague that
is believed to have been spread by fleas on rats.
It swept through Europe in the fourteenth century,
arriving in England in 1348, where it killed
over one third of the population.

One of the Black Death's main symptoms was
**foul-smelling boils all over the body called
'buboes'.** The plague was so infectious that its
victims and their families were locked in their houses
until they died. Many villages were abandoned as
the disease wiped out their populations.

So many people died that graveyards overflowed
and bodies lay in the street, so special **'plague pits'**
were dug to bury the bodies. Almost every town
and village in England has a plague pit
somewhere underneath it, so watch out
when you're digging in the garden . . .

Dear Reader

As you may have already guessed, B. Strange is not a real name.

The author of this series is an ex-teacher who is currently employed by a little-known body called the Organisation For Spook Termination (Excluding Demons), or O.F.S.T.(E.D.). 'B. Strange' is the pen name chosen to protect his identity.

Together, we felt it was our duty to publish these books, in an attempt to save innocent lives. The stories are based on the author's experiences as an O.F.S.T.(E.D.) inspector in various schools over the past two decades.

Please read them carefully - you may regret it if you don't . . .

Yours sincerely
The Publisher.

PS - Should you wish to file a report on any suspicious supernatural occurrences at your school, visit **www.too-ghoul.com** and fill out the relevant form. We'll pass it on to O.F.S.T.(E.D.) for you.

PPS - All characters' names have been changed to protect the identity of the individuals. Any similarity to actual persons, living or undead, is purely coincidental.

CONTENTS

CHAPTER 1
LOST IN TRANSLATION

James chewed on his pen, frowning.

'I can't do this!' he groaned. He threw the pen down on to the desk with a clatter.

Alexander looked up. He'd written three pages of a letter to his French pen pal already. Unlike James's scribbles, Alexander's page was neat and tidy, just like him.

'Here, James,' said Alexander, holding out a huge, leather-bound book, 'you can use my French dictionary. I got it for my birthday last year. I was really excited, because I'd always wanted . . .'

'Only you'd ask for a dictionary for your birthday!' James spluttered. 'Thanks, though. I'm having real trouble with this letter,' he sighed, grabbing the book from his friend and beginning to leaf through it.

It was Monday morning, and Madame Dupont – St Sebastian's French teacher – had instructed her year-sevens to fill their pen pals in on their latest news. She liked using the double lesson first thing on a Monday morning for this, as it meant she could ease her way in to the new week by drinking strong black coffee and reading her French newspaper in peace. She imagined she was sitting in a café in Paris rather than in her stuffy classroom at St Sebastian's.

Alexander signed his letter with a flourish and leant back in his chair, flexing his knuckles and stretching. James looked up.

'Well, that's this month's letter to Isabelle sorted out,' smiled Alexander. 'I can't *wait* to hear back from her. I've asked her lots of questions about the French government. She mentioned that her father works in an incredibly interesting department that organises payments for farmers –'

'Stick?' James interrupted.

'Yes, James?'

'Some of us haven't finished. And exciting as I am *sure* Isabelle's dad's job sounds – *not!* – I have to get this done before break time.' He scrubbed at his hair with frustration, leaving it sticking out like a punky hedgehog.

'Sorry, James! Here – let me help,' Alexander replied, leaning over to see what James had written. His brow furrowed. He scratched his head.

'It gives me the creeps when you scratch like that. Makes me think there are zombie nits on your bonce!' shuddered James.

'Have no fear, I'm a nit-free zone!' declared Alexander. He looked at James's letter and started to laugh.

'What's so funny?' James asked, frowning.

'Erm . . . did you mean to say "I like to ride my fish committee?"' Alexander spluttered.

Madame Dupont looked up from her newspaper. 'Alexandre? Is there a problem?'

'No, no – just helping the less fortunate!' Alexander giggled.

Madame Dupont smiled. 'Very well, Alexandre! Carry on!' She took a slurp of her coffee and went back to her newspaper.

James poked Alexander. 'What are you going on about? I was just telling Zac about my skateboard. I even used your stupid dictionary. I looked up "skate", then I looked up "board" and I put them together to make "skateboard". Simple. So I don't know why you're getting your knickers in a twist.'

'Well, you looked up "skate" and got the word for a type of flat fish, like a ray. Then you looked up "board" and you got the type of board that's a committee – like the board of school governors. Mind you, in a way, you're not far off the mark . . . when Dad talks to the governors I've seen them opening and closing their mouths like fish . . .'

'Oh, this is just stupid!' James snorted. 'I'll just draw a picture of me on my skateboard instead.'

'But Madame Dupont wants us to –' Alexander began. He was silenced by a glare from James. He swallowed hard and turned to Lenny, who was attaching some fluff to his letter with a piece of sticky tape.

'What's that?' Alexander asked.

'It was stuck in the zip of my pencil case. It's a clump of fur off our cat Cleo. She likes to sleep in my schoolbag, where it's dark and warm. Sometimes she leaves bits of herself behind . . .' He rummaged about in his bag and brought out a bent whisker. 'See!' He taped that to his letter too.

'OK . . . but why are you sticking it to your letter?' asked Alexander.

'Well, I was telling my pen pal, Manu, about the things my pets have been getting up to. I told him about the time my hamster escaped and hid in Mum's jewellery box. When she opened the lid, there was Leo wearing one of her bracelets like a necklace! I can't understand why she screamed. She scared the life out of him. And I also told him about the time Pooza the rabbit –'

'*Pooza*?' Alexander interrupted. 'What kind of name is that?!'

'Well, my mum said I should give my animals names that suit their personalities and habits,' Lenny smiled. 'And that rabbit poos – a *lot*. His cage is always full of piles of rabbit raisins. I have to clear him out twice a week – so that's how he earnt his name!'

'*Ewww* – too much information!' Alexander laughed, screwing up his nose.

'Anyway, I was just telling Manu about how Cleo likes to sleep in my schoolbag, when I suddenly had an idea. I wanted Manu to understand all about my pets, so that's why I stuck a bit of fluff on my letter.'

'Hey – it's a good job Pooza's not here. I don't think Manu would have liked rabbit raisins taped to his letter!'

The boys tried to stifle their laughter.

Madame Dupont looked up at that moment, but they were saved by the school bell. Everyone began to cram books into their schoolbags.

Madame Dupont clapped her hands to get attention. 'Wait a minute, please, everyone! I have an exciting announcement to make!'

'Free *pain au chocolat* for everyone?' wondered Alexander, hopefully.

'Don't be daft, Stick! What use would a chocolate pan be? It'd be as useless as a chocolate teapot. No good for cooking . . .' Lenny frowned.

'No, not a chocolate pan – *pain au chocolat*!

We had them on holiday last year. They're flaky pastry with chocolate chips – yum!' Alexander smiled, wistfully. His tummy rumbled.

'I have arranged a pupil exchange with L'Ecole de St Martin, your pen pals' school in Poubelle! You will all finally get to meet your French friends – next week!' trilled Madame Dupont, beaming at her pupils with excitement.

The boys looked at each other in silence. Then they grinned.

'Wow! A school trip to France!' cried James. 'Brilliant! I've always fancied . . .'

'Sorry, James. We are going nowhere. The students from L'Ecole de St Martin are to come here,' Madame Dupont smiled.

James deflated like a burst balloon.

'Aww, Madame Dupont . . .!' he moaned.

'I shall give you all more details very soon! Now I must go to make arrangements . . .' And with a waft of her chiffon scarf – leaving a trail

9

10

of expensive perfume in her wake – the French mistress swept out of the classroom.

James turned to Lenny and Alexander. 'You can always trust a teacher to suck the fun out of things!' he grumbled.

'Cheer up, James! It'll be great. We'll be able to show them around Grimesford . . .' said Alexander.

'And Manu will be able to meet my pets!' Lenny grinned.

'Hmm, well, I suppose I'll be able to show Zac my skateboard. He could even come to the skatepark,' said James, perking up a bit.

'You know, I've got a theory why teachers suck all the fun out of things,' said Alexander. 'Do you want to hear it?'

James sighed and crossed his arms. 'No, I don't – but I've got a horrible feeling I'm going to anyway.'

'Because somewhere along the line they've been crossed with vampires.'

'Eh?' James grunted. 'I'm not sure I get where this is going . . .'

'And do you know what you get if you cross a teacher with a vampire?'

James and Lenny silently exchanged puzzled glances.

'Someone who likes to do a lot of blood tests!' Alexander laughed.

His friends rolled their eyes and groaned, and the boys pushed and jostled with each other as they headed out of the classroom to the playground.

CHAPTER 2
WHOSE NEWS?

It was the end of assembly the next day and everyone had begun to fidget and shuffle. Lenny stretched his long legs out to try and un-kink them, while James lifted each of his buttocks off his chair in turn to try and relieve the pins and needles in his bum.

'And finally, I have some *excellent* news!' said Mr Tick, the headmaster, rubbing his hands together and grinning like a well-fed hyena. 'We are having visitors from another school in Poubelle, France! As you all know, I am totally dedicated to building bridges with our European neighbours.' He beamed and stroked his lapels of his smart pinstripe jacket.

James leant in towards Lenny. 'He does realise they're school kids like us, doesn't he? I've never noticed him make us feel welcome – and it's our school!'

Lenny pulled a face. Alexander turned at that moment, his face shining brightly as he listened to his dad, Mr Tick. His smile slipped when he saw Lenny's face.

'What's up?' he mouthed.

'Um ... er ... trapped wind, Stick. Giving me a bellyache,' Lenny said, thinking quickly.

Alexander smiled.

'Not like you to have a problem letting one go, Lenny!' James hissed.

'To make absolutely sure that our French friends feel at home,' Mr Tick smiled, smugly, 'I have had a *splendid* idea, if I do say so myself.'

He flicked back his fringe with his fingers and polished his nails on his jacket. 'I have personally arranged for the canteen to serve French food – and *only* French food – for the duration of their visit!' He beamed around the hall as though he expected a round of applause. Madame Dupont stiffened and stared at the headmaster. Her eyebrows shot up and her mouth fell open in a silent 'o'.

James nudged Lenny. 'Not sure it was Mr Tick's idea after all!' he whispered. By now, Madame Dupont had crossed her arms angrily and was shaking her head. The headmaster carried on regardless.

'So, we have some *haute cuisine* to look forward to next week!'

Lenny frowned. 'Hot kweeseen? What's that?' he whispered.

Alexander turned around and touched his fingers to his lips.

'Shh! It means "fine cooking",' he hissed. 'I think he's got something else to tell us . . .'

Mr Tick clasped his hands together.

'And there's more! As a special treat, all year-seven lessons will be France-focused!' Once again, he beamed out at the assembled pupils and staff.

'Eh?' said Lenny, screwing up his face. 'What's he on about?'

'He means,' sighed Alexander, 'that we'll be studying French history, French music, and so on.' He nudged his friend's arm. 'Come on, Lenny – it'll be fun!'

Meanwhile, Madame Dupont was muttering in French under her breath.

'Look!' James hissed. 'Looks like Madame Dupont is ready to blow a fuse! I think it might have been her idea, and Mr Tick is taking the credit . . .'

Alexander turned around again and frowned.

'Shhh! I want to hear what Dad's got to say. He's got some great ideas today!' As he turned away, James shrugged at Lenny.

Finally, assembly finished and everyone filed out the hall. Lenny turned to James.

'I'm still a bit worried about this hot kweeseen, James,' he said. James grinned.

'I wouldn't let it bother you, Lenny. If I know Mrs Cooper and Mrs Meadows, the kitchens will still be producing all the old favourites – and there'll always be *pommes frites* on the menu!'

'Pom whats?' asked Lenny.

'Chips to you and me, Lenny!' laughed James, flinging an arm around his confused friend's shoulder as they headed to their first lesson.

CHAPTER 3
A LUKEWARM RECEPTION

James, Lenny and Alexander stood in the school
car park. The day of the school visit had arrived,
and the year-sevens were waiting for their pen
pals. A chilly wind whistled round them,
whipping crisp and sweet wrappers up in tiny
litter whirlwinds. James batted at a toffee wrapper
as it slapped at his cheek. Lenny tugged at the
neck of his stripy jumper.

'This is itchy! Why did we have to dress up
like this anyway?' he grumbled.

James scowled. 'I know – we look like humbugs

in this get-up!' he groaned. Alexander frowned.

'Well, it was Dad's idea – you know, to make our pen pals feel at home,' he explained.

'Yeah, but doesn't he know that French people only wear stripy tops in cartoons, not in real life? He's made us look like a right bunch of idiots!'

'Listen, children!' Madame Dupont called. 'Our

visitors will be here soon. I just got a call on my mobile from the group organiser. Their coach has left Cricklebrooke, where our friends are staying in a hotel, so they are on their way. It is exciting, *non*?' she smiled.

'I'd vote *non* all right. I'm frozen and I feel like a right fool standing here dressed up like a French onion seller!' moaned James. At that moment, a strange roaring noise came from the bottom of the school drive.

'What was that?' gasped Alexander, wide-eyed.

'Sounds like a dragon with pneumonia!' laughed James.

A large coach chugged towards the school. The paintwork was chipped and the windows were scratched and dirty.

'More like a clapped-out old dinosaur!' Alexander smirked.

'Look, children! My beloved French flag is in the back window!' Madame Dupont trilled, happily.

'Blimey! That wreck's so old, I'm surprised it's not being pulled by horses!' said Lenny, pointing to the back of the bus.

A huge cloud of dirty grey smoke gushed from the boot into the cold air. With a loud belch and an explosive cough, the engine juddered to a halt.

'Excuse me!' James joked, wafting at his own bottom. Madame Dupont paused her flag-waving long enough to glare at James.

'You know, that smoke looks a bit weird,' said James, rubbing his eyes. 'For a moment there, I thought I could see horrible ghostly *faces* in it.' He shook his head. 'I must be losing it!' he laughed, nervously.

The thick smoke coiled across the car park, its fingers creeping under the door of the boiler house and sliding down into the drains.

The French pupils stared sullenly out of the windows of the coach.

The St Sebastian's year-sevens stared back.

23

A fine, misty rain began to fall. It blew in grey sheets across the car park.

James shook his head. Drips of water plopped off his fringe and ran into his eyes.

'Could this get any worse?' he wondered aloud.

At that moment, Madame Dupont began to sing the French national anthem in a loud, shrill voice. As she warbled on, her eyeliner began to run down her face.

'Sing, children, sing!' she urged, desperately trying to save the situation.

'In answer to my own question: yes – it just did!' James grumbled to himself.

The French children stumbled down the steps of the coach and stood shivering in the rain.

Madame Dupont quickly pulled out a clipboard and started to read from her list of pupils.

'Let's get you all in pairs quickly, *non*? Then we can get out of this awful rain – I'm sure this wasn't the sort of English greeting our visitors were expecting.' Her French colleagues smiled weakly.

'James? Here is Zac . . . come, come, say "*bonjour*", James. Lenny? Meet Emmanuel. Alexandre, this is Isabelle . . . where is Alexandre?' The teacher quickly matched all the French and English pupils with one another.

James smiled awkwardly at Zac. Lenny and Emmanuel eyed each other suspiciously. Alexander extended his hand towards Isabelle.

'*Bonjour*, Isabelle.' The girl smiled shyly and gave Alexander a little wave in response.

By now, Madame Dupont had linked arms with two of the St Martin's teachers and they were heading towards the main entrance, chatting.

'Listen to them!' James hissed. 'They sound like a bunch of hens clucking away.'

'French hens, of course!' Alexander laughed. His friends groaned as they all followed the teachers into the school.

Down in the sewer, a strange troupe of ragged ghosts drifted along the tunnels. They were led by a tall phantom in gleaming silver armour. He marched along in front, waving his sword.

'The main chamber – how did that young ghost call it? The amphitheatre? It must be close now. The boy he said it is *magnifique*!' the knight roared.

A runty little man-servant spectre scurried along beside him.

'And you are the ghost to rule it, *oui*?' he simpered. The knight grinned. His huge, grey teeth looked like gravestones in the dim light.

'*Oui!* And I will not rest until I am the lord of all!'

CHAPTER 4
TALL, DARK AND SLIMY

'Come along, hurry up! I have places to go and people to haunt, you know!' Edith Codd – self-appointed leader of the ghosts who lived under St Sebastian's School – clapped her knobbly hands together. 'I've called you together because I have something very important to say!'

Ghosts trailed into the gloomy amphitheatre. Candle flames flickered in the alcoves on the wall. A fat, hairy spider dangled down from the ceiling in front of Edith's face like a pendulum. She swatted at it, and it shot across the heads of the assembled ghosts like a party streamer.

William Scroggins, the ghost of a small, thin boy, caught the spider and popped it safely down his collar. It crept up his neck and settled comfortably in his ear.

'Oh! You've got a new friend, William!' smiled Lady Grimes, an elegant ghost dressed in velvet. She patted William's shoulder.

Ambrose Harbottle, a ghostly leech merchant, sat next to her. He was rummaging in a tin of leeches. Picking out a fat, black creature that pulsed in his hand, he popped it into his mouth and started to chew happily. He grinned at William, exposing teeth coated in grey slime.

'Wonder what the old trout wants now?' he pondered.

Edith smashed her fist down hard on the upturned barrel she used as a ranting post.

'Order! Order!' she screeched.

A rat shrieked and shot out of an alcove.

Confused by the noise, it leapt straight into the ghost witch Aggie Malkin and tangled in her long, matted hair. She reached up and stroked the rodent gently.

'Oh, dear, my pretty, did that nasty Edith scare you? Don't worry, Aggie will take care of you!' She tickled the rat's hairy tummy and it settled down for a nap.

Lilith Skitterpaws, Aggie's fierce cat, eyed it hungrily. Aggie swatted her on the tail and she hissed. Bertram Ruttle, the plague pit's resident musician, was sitting nearby. The cat ran up his trouser leg, shredding it completely. He cried out in surprise and leapt up, dropping his bone xylophone with a clatter.

'Oh, for goodness' sake!' Edith shouted angrily. 'Listen! I have very important news! I hope everyone's here; I've noticed several ghosts missing from my meetings lately, and I shall *not* tolerate it!' As she worked herself up into a frenzy, flecks of spittle gathered on her thin lips and flew into the air. A blob landed on William's cheek and he scrubbed at it with his hand in disgust.

Edith glanced around the amphitheatre. It was crammed with even more ghosts than usual, she noticed. She smiled grimly.

That annoying ghost Ambrose is sitting on the floor with that horrible child William because there aren't enough seats! she thought, and beamed smugly. *That'll teach them to come in late. Everyone must be here today!*

'Right. I have noticed recently that St Sebastian's School has become even more horribly noisy than usual. There seem to be more p . . . p . . . pupils,' she spat on the floor, 'in the school than ever. I don't know the reason, but I mean to find out – and that's where you miserable lot come in. I can't be everywhere at once, so you will have to be my eyes and ears!'

'Yuck! I wouldn't want to be one of her eyes!'

Ambrose grimaced. 'They're like mouldy old eggs!'

William tittered. 'Her ears aren't much better either,' he whispered. 'They look like the slimy old graveyard fungus!'

Ambrose laughed so hard that he snorted.

Edith narrowed her eyes and peered into the crowd. 'This is no laughing matter!' she scowled. At the front, she saw a tall, dark, handsome ghost in shining armour staring back at her.

Hmm . . . where have you been all my afterlife? she wondered.

The stranger smiled warmly, winked at her, then blew her a kiss. Edith pulled at her collar coyly and patted her wiry, red hair.

I haven't seen him before . . . still, I suppose there must be hundreds of ghosts from the plague pit down here. It's quite possible I've just been too busy to notice him. Edith brushed some slime off her dress and pulled herself together. Her ectoplasm had begun to smoke at the sight of the handsome stranger.

'We *must* find out what's going on and put a stop to it! We cannot have all this noise and disturbance! We must rid St Sebastian's of this plague of children!' she continued.

'Plague? Where?' a small, scared-looking ghost squealed and ran from the amphitheatre.

Edith rolled her eyes. 'Oh, for goodness' sake . . . just get out there, everybody, and find out what's going on!'

The ghosts gradually drifted from the cavern, grumbling and moaning. Edith pushed and shoved at them to hurry them along. Somebody stood close to her and, as she turned to snarl, he put his hand on hers.

'*Bonjour*, Edith. Hello, pretty lady! *Je m'appelle* . . . how you say? My name is Count Maurice.' He bowed before the old hag, kissing her flaky hand.

Her eyes goggled and she stared at the tall, dark ghost, then down at her hand, as though she'd never seen it before.

'It is always a pleasure to meet a lovely lady!' he gushed.

Ambrose was on his way past when he screeched to a halt at the sound of this.

'*Lovely*'? '*Lady*'? – *Edith?!* He thought, poking a finger into his ear and wiggling it backwards and forwards. He pulled out a huge blob of earwax, popped it in his mouth, and chewed. Suddenly, Edith let out a high-pitched giggle, making Ambrose jump.

'Nothing wrong with my hearing then!' he muttered. '"Lovely" – Edith!' he scoffed. 'The man must be mad!'

'Yuck!' said William, making a face. 'Is he blind or daft?'

By now Maurice was holding Edith's hand. He gave it back and tickled her cheek. A line of maggots trickled from one of her eye sockets and fell on to the back of his hand. He nibbled them as he whispered sweet nothings into her scabby ear.

'Edith, your skin, it is the colour of a rotten death shroud. Your lips, they are like twin grave worms glistening in the candlelight . . .'

William shuddered. Ambrose frowned.

'You know, William, there's something fishy going on here. I've never seen that fella before, have you? And it's not just him. It's his mates, too. Do any of them look familiar to you, son?' William shook his head.

'We've been down here six hundred years and we managed to miss them all this time? – I don't think so. There's definitely something going on here, lad . . .'

CHAPTER 5
POMMES FRIGHTS

The next day, James, Lenny and Alexander were walking to school together.

'Well, at least they're not staying overnight with us too!' huffed James. 'It's hard enough work at school!'

'Tell me about it!' said Lenny, rolling his eyes. 'I keep trying to talk to Manu, but it's just too difficult. I can't make him understand me, even if I talk really loudly and slowly . . .'

Alexander slapped his own forehead. 'He's French, not stupid, Lenny!'

36

'Whatever,' Lenny shrugged. 'All I know is I just can't get through to Manu. Last night, when he came round for tea, I showed him my animals. I took him out to the shed to see that injured hedgehog I'm looking after – you know, Spike. I picked her up and held her up close to him so he could pet her, and all he did was hold his nose and say "poo!" So I showed him my crow with the wonky wing instead. You remember Eric, yeah? He's starting to get better and flaps about all over the place and everything now. But he turned his nose up at Eric, too! Would you believe it?' Lenny shook his head. 'So I gave up trying to get him interested in Roland . . .'

'That would be the rat, right?' James smiled.

'Yup – the one with the gammy leg. He's getting much better now. Anyway, when we went to my room to play *Zombie Strike 4 – Mall of the Dead* on the computer, our cat Cleo was asleep on the bed. What did Manu do? He only started sneezing, didn't he. The poor cat was terrified! I just don't think that boy relates to animals!'

Alexander patted Lenny's shoulder.

'Nobody quite understands them the way you do, Lenny! But never mind. My evening didn't go well either, if it's any consolation. Isabelle's nice enough, but she's really, really shy. She can understand me all right, but she just nods and smiles. I even translated loads of jokes into French for her – but nothing! They didn't raise a titter!'

'Jokes . . . into French?' James shook his head. 'Only you, Stick!'

'I told her some of my favourites, too!' grumbled Alexander.

'Like what?' asked Lenny.

'The one about maths teachers and sweets,' replied Alexander.

'Go on then . . . try it on us!' Lenny smiled.

'OK – what are maths teachers' favourite sweets?'

'No idea – amaze us!' said James.

'Measure-mints!' laughed Alexander. James staggered backwards.

'No wonder she didn't laugh . . . that's *awful*!' he groaned. 'I reckon she's just acting shy cos she's been landed with you!'

'Well, at least I'm making an effort!' Alexander frowned.

'Hey, I'm trying too!' James protested. 'I took Zac to the skatepark. He was pretty good on the skateboard but we had to keep making signs at each other instead of talking. It was all pretty confusing. I tried to ask if he wanted to go and get some chips but I just gave up in the end.'

The boys had reached the school gates.

'Here we go!' James sighed. 'Another confusing day begins!'

When the lunch bell rang, the friends – and their pen pals – made their way to the canteen. The room was decorated with red, blue and white streamers and balloons. Mr Wharpley, the school caretaker, pushed past them angrily, carrying a stepladder.

'Flaming balloons . . . flaming streamers . . . flaming kids!' he muttered.

'Looks like someone's happy to see the visitors,' whispered James, sarcastically.

The children lined up at the counter to be served. Lynn Cooper was slopping dollops of grey potato on to plates. Sue Meadows was serving up great, steaming scoops of chips from a tin tray dripping with grease and labelled *pommes frites* in biro on a torn packet top.

'Ah, excellent – business as usual!' Lenny beamed. 'Double chips, please, Mrs Meadows.' The dinner lady piled his plate high.

'Those *croques-monsieurs* don't look too

appetising!' James giggled, pointing to the soggy-looking melted cheese concoctions. 'And those pancakes look horrible!' He pointed, wrinkling up his nose. Zac sniggered.

'Not pancakes, James – *crêpes*!' corrected Alexander.

James poked one of the limp-looking desserts.

'Hmm, what they look like sounds like "*crêpe*"!' he snorted, nudging Isabelle.

They all found an empty table and sat down.

'So, what's St Martin's like, Zac? It must be better than this dump,' said James. Alexander shot him a look. 'I'm not getting at your dad! Not really . . .' he protested.

Zac looked puzzled.

'A little help here, Stick? Come on!' pleaded James.

Alexander translated and Zac looked away. He blinked and glanced at Manu and Isabelle, sighing heavily. Then he began to tell his story.

'St Martin . . . she is . . . it is . . . *mal, très mal!*' He looked at James with huge, haunted eyes.

'*Mal?* What does *mal* mean?' James asked, looking from Zac to Alexander and back again.

'And where does the "tray" come in?' Lenny asked, looking baffled.

'Well, *mal* means "bad",' Alexander said. He

turned to Lenny. 'And *très* means "very". So there must be something badly wrong at St Martins!'

Isabelle scowled and clicked her tongue against her teeth. She put her hand on Zac's arm and shook her head.

'What's she so scared of?' James asked.

'It is nothing,' she said in a quiet voice.

James rubbed his chin. He turned to Lenny and Alexander.

'Hmm, OK – I'll just have to ask Zac when he's on his own and see what I can find out. I don't like the sound of this. Not one bit . . .'

CHAPTER 6
THE TERRIBLE TRUTH

That afternoon, the year-sevens were on the sports field waiting to play rounders. The St Sebastian's and St Martin's pupils stood in two separate camps, eyeing each other with suspicion.

'Right, James – you can be captain of one team; Eleanor – you be captain of the other team. Now, choose your players!' said Ms Legg, as she jogged up and down the field enthusiastically.

James took a deep breath and blew his cheeks out noisily. 'Lenny.' The tall boy walked across and joined him.

'Isabelle,' Eleanor smiled.

The French girl grinned bashfully at Eleanor and walked across to stand beside her. By now, Alexander was bobbing from foot to foot, looking eagerly at James.

'Yes – you, Stick,' James sighed.

Alexander beamed and trotted across to join his friends, tripping on his laces on the way and landing in a heap. James shook his head slowly. 'Great start . . .' he muttered, sighing again.

'Luke?' Eleanor asked a tall, slim boy. He grinned and wandered across.

'Zac?' James asked.

Zac nodded and joined the boys.

'It'll be a chance for us to find out a bit more about St Martin's!' James whispered to his friends. 'And since Isabelle's on the other team, she won't be able to stop him!'

Once the teams were chosen, the players collected bats and bases and walked out on to the pitch. James made sure he was fielding right next to Zac, so as to give him a grilling about St Martin's.

'Zac, you know you said your school was bad? *Mal*? What did you mean?'

Zac shuddered and rubbed his arms. 'We are happy to be away from St Martin's because the things *plus strange* – very strange – happen there all the day.'

James frowned, confused. 'What do you mean, "strange"? We've got some pretty weird teachers – is that what you mean?' he asked, fishing for more information.

'*Non*. It is far, far stranger than anything the teachers do or say – and some of them are . . .' he pointed his finger at his forehead and circled it round and round. Then he stopped to think for a moment and waved his arms in front of him. 'It is whoooo! How you say? *Fantôme!*'

Just as the truth finally hit home to James,

a rounders ball hit him equally hard on the arm
with a 'thunk'.

'Ow! Blimey! Ow!' he howled, clutching his
arm.

'Sorry, James!' Alexander panted as he ran towards him. 'I was trying to get Eleanor out but I hit you with the ball instead of hitting the base!'

Monsieur Leblanc, one of the teachers from St Martin's, jogged up to the boys.

'You are well, yes?' he asked.

'Yeah, it's just Alexander's a bit of a danger to public safety when he plays sport . . .' James laughed. Alexander blushed and looked down. 'Don't worry, Stick, it's OK,' he smiled, rubbing the bruise.

'*Bien*. Good. Right. Well, if there was less chatting and more eyes on the ball, perhaps you would not have been bashed, yes?' the French teacher smiled.

'Yes . . . no . . .' James nodded, confused.

'Spread out on the field, boys! Come on, hurry up!' Ms Legg called.

'Later . . .' James whispered to Zac. The boy nodded and they jogged out to finish the game.

Back in the boys' changing room after the match, the boys continued their conversation.

'So, ghosts, you say?' James asked.

Zac looked around him to check no one was listening. '*Oui* – yes – ghosts! They jump out of the cupboards, they mess with our food, they attack us when we study. It is most terrible!'

'Sounds familiar!' James nodded.

Zac frowned. 'Eh? Who else has talked?' he asked, confused.

'Hang on, mate – Lenny! Alexander! Come here and listen to this!' James called over the noise in the changing room.

The boys rushed across, still pulling on their uniforms as they went.

'Tell them what you told me, Zac!' said James.

Zac shrugged and told the boys his story.

By the time he'd finished, Lenny's mouth was hanging open. Alexander looked stunned.

'So, I am glad to be here for a rest from all of the spooky goings-on!' Zac smiled, uncertainly.

'Erm, I'm not sure how to tell you this,' James said, patting Zac on the shoulder. 'But I think you have jumped from the frying pan into the fire!'

Zac jumped and looked around, terrified. 'Fire? Where? What pan?'

'Sorry, Zac!' James smiled. 'It's just an English saying. It means things have gone from bad to worse.'

Zac just stared at James. 'I do not understand . . .'

'Well, it's like this, mate. St Sebastian's is haunted too!'

Zac's shoulders sagged and his face fell.

'Hey – you look like you've been hit by something heavy!' said Lenny.

'He has,' Alexander sighed. 'The knowledge that there are spectres and wraiths at St

51

Sebastian's is a heavy load for us all to bear . . .'

'Eh?' said Lenny and Zac at the same time.
They grinned at each other.

'Don't worry!' Lenny laughed. 'I speak English
and I still can't understand him half the time!'

Alexander scowled.

'You know what I mean. There are ghosts here
– and it's horrible!'

'Well, why didn't you just *say* that?' said Lenny,
folding his arms.

'I thought I had . . .' Alexander protested.

'Anyway,' interrupted James, 'it sounds as though
we've got the same problem. Sometimes it feels as
though there's a ghastly ghoul up to no good
everywhere you turn here!' His friends nodded in
agreement. Zac paled. 'But the strange thing is,
people must walk round with blinkers on – or
blindfolds! Only a few people know the truth.'

'Ah, well, you see, James, *I* think they're in
denial,' lectured Alexander. 'People know there

are ghosts, but they refused to *accept* that knowledge because it doesn't fit with their perception of the world. Therefore –'

'All right, professor! Can we get back to the important part of all this?' James grumbled. Alexander's mouth fell shut. 'There's no need to worry, Zac. We keep our ghosts firmly under control here.'

Lenny looked at Alexander and raised his eyebrows.

CHAPTER 7
LOVE IS BLIND

Down in the sewer, Edith and Count Maurice went everywhere together. If she sat down, he sat beside her. If she wandered around the amphitheatre, he was like a puppy following behind her. Edith loved it. She kept gazing at him, her red eyes gleaming.

'Is it just me, or do those two turn your stomach?' Ambrose asked William, putting a hand on his stomach and releasing a small, fetid burp.

William wrinkled his nose. 'It's horrible, Ambrose. And a bit strange. I mean, why would

Maurice be so interested in Edith? She's . . . erm, well . . .' William struggled to find a polite way to describe her.

'A wizened old hag with a face like a dead badger's backside?' Ambrose suggested, helpfully.

'*Exactly!*' William giggled.

At that moment, Edith swept past, with Maurice stuck to her side like a limpet.

'I heard about you from far away across the sea, *ma chérie!*' he gushed. 'Your leadership skills are legendary and, of course, you are famed for your dazzling beauty. Your eyes, they are like deep, fiery pools . . .'

'Cess pools, more like!' Ambrose hissed.

By now, William was squirming with the effort of holding back his laughter. But Edith didn't even notice – she was too busy gazing into Maurice's eyes.

'We have travelled many miles and for endless days just to see you with our own eyes. We wanted to join you here in your charming – how you say? – pit. It is good, yes?' Maurice smarmed.

'Oh, yes!' Edith sighed. Her rancid breath rushed across a cloud of passing flies. They stiffened and dropped to the ground one by one like tiny fighter planes.

Ambrose poked William sharply. 'Look over there! What's going on?'

A group of ghosts he didn't recognise were building some kind of structure from the skeletons of the plague victims. Bertram Ruttle was storming about, grabbing bones and pushing the strange ghosts out of the way.

'These are my private property! I'll thank you not to steal them. Ugh! They're all sticky! What *have* you been doing with them?'

A snooty French ghost looked down his nose at him.

'Remove your hand, peasant! Nobody touches *Le Pimpernel* and lives to tell the tale!' The ghost shot backwards and drew a sword.

Unfortunately, the swift movement caused him to drop the skull he was holding in his other hand.

'Don't lose your head!' Bertram laughed, kicking it across the amphitheatre. While the ghost stumbled after it, cursing, he grabbed more bones and thrust them into a stained sack.

Ambrose shuffled over to his friend, who was busily grabbing armfuls of ribs and finger bones.

'What's going on, Bertram?' he asked. He picked up a bone. 'This sticky stuff is good old sewer sludge. I'd know it anywhere – leeches love it!' His mouth fell open in disbelief as he came round to the front of the structure. 'It's a flaming statue of that Maurice! I don't believe it! The cheek!'

'Oh, yes,' Bertram growled. 'Haven't you noticed? He thinks he owns the place!'

'If things carry on like this, he soon will!' Ambrose said, pointing at Edith and Maurice. They were sitting close together, whispering to one another. Ambrose crept closer to listen.

'You know, Edith, you are already my phantom queen, with your great beauty. Your teeth, they glisten like the maggots, yes? And your hair, it is like the matted horse tails.' Maurice whispered. 'But you are such a glorious leader that you should rule the entire school! You burn far too brightly to be contained in this small sewer! You should be on show, glittering jewel of the grave that you are. You should storm the barricades and take over the school! Declare yourself queen of all you see!'

Edith was blown away by the French knight's flattery. She picked happily at the flakes of skin dangling from her nose. *At last, a man who truly understands me*, she thought to herself, popping the flakes in her mouth and crunching.

Ambrose tore his gaze away from Edith and Maurice, and looked round the amphitheatre. Two strange French ghosts were emptying Aggie Malkin's alcove. They carried bag after bag of potions and spell books down the sewer. Another strange ghost was organising a collection of tattered French cushions in the corner of the amphitheatre. He looked up and blew a kiss at Lady Grimes as she passed by. She ignored the compliment. Ambrose scowled. Then the French ghost plumped up his last cushion and propped up a sign saying 'No peasants! By order of Count Maurice of Poubelle'.

'William!' Ambrose shouted.

William scurried across to where Ambrose was standing.

'We have to do something!' Ambrose hissed. 'These French ghosts are taking over the sewer. This is outrageous!' He grabbed hold of Lady Grimes's hand as she passed, and she smiled.

'Are you all right, my love?' he asked, anxiously.

'Of course, Ambrose!' Lady Grimes chuckled. 'You know I only have eyes for you!' And to prove it, she opened her hand and showed him her eyeballs. 'See?'

Ambrose grinned.

At that moment, there was a terrible shrieking sound. Lilith Skitterpaws, Aggie's cat, had come into the amphitheatre and had seen her mistress's belongings being thrown into a corner. Worse still, some ghost she did not recognise was dragging her nice, comfy cat bed towards the fire!

The cat pounced on the offending ghost, puncturing his bottom with her steely claws. He screamed and leapt into the air, scattering spell books and a rather nasty-looking bottle of potion on to the floor. The bottle broke, and a shimmering cloud of purple dust filled the air. Slowly, a pointy-nosed genie took shape. It had green skin and hypnotic, yellow eyes.

'Who dares disturb the rest of Maroth the Magnificent?' it bellowed.

The ghost who had dropped the bottle tried to hide under Lilith's cat bed, but she was waiting. She raked her sharp claws down his face and chewed on the ectoplasm that squirted from the wounds. The genie swept towards the ghost, who scrambled from the cat's clutches and took off at speed down the corridor.

Edith didn't even look up. She was lost, gazing into Maurice's eyes.

'Is she spellbound?' William asked.

'She will be when Aggie Malkin finds her stuff all over the place and that genie loose in the sewer!' said Ambrose. 'Look – they're still whispering together. It's enough to make you sick! William, sneak a bit closer and see what they're talking about, there's a good lad.'

William crept closer to the ghostly lovebirds. His lip curled in disgust as he saw Maurice stroke Edith's wiry hair. A clump fell out and he tied it round his wrist.

'At least agree to come above with me. Then we shall see how I can take ov– I mean, you can take your rightful place as Empress Edith!' Maurice said, slimily.

Edith patted her hair and gave a little smile. 'Well, you know, I have this rule that nobody makes themselves visible to the staff and pupils unless they are attacking the school . . .' she began.

'Invisible? *You*? That would be a crime! Your corpse-like beauty would make the living pale by comparison – your ragged dress, your frizzy hair and your beautiful, stained teeth . . . I will collect my things and a shawl for your pretty shoulders, *ma petite*. Just a moment.' Maurice wandered across to the pile of cushions and picked up a piece of rotting lace.

'Ick! Looking at Edith this close makes *me* go pale all right,' William said to himself. He scuttled back to Ambrose before Edith noticed him.

'They're planning to go up top!' William hissed.

'But Edith never risks wandering about the school unless she's on the attack!' Ambrose whispered. He shambled over to Edith.

'You're not going up to the school, are you?

63

What if someone sees you, and they get an exorcist in?' he said, trying to deter her.

'Oh, Ambrose – you silly man! What harm could possibly come to me with Maurice by my side? It is nice of you to care – and lovely to be fought over by *two* men . . .' her hand fluttered at her throat. Ambrose looked as though he had been hit with a brick.

'*Fighting?*' he muttered. 'No, Edith, you don't understand. This Maurice and his merry band – they're up to something! I think they mean to take over the sewer – look around you!'

Edith glanced around the amphitheatre.

'Whatever gave you that idea? They've just made a few improvements, that's all. Don't worry!' she patted him on the hand. He whipped it back as though he had been bitten by a snake.

Maurice returned with the shawl and draped it around Edith's shoulders. He pushed Ambrose out of the way and steered her towards the pipes that

would take them up to the school above.

As Ambrose glared after them, Maurice turned and sneered, his eyes glittering evilly.

CHAPTER 8
KNIGHT IN SHINING ARMOUR

James rolled his eyes. 'Is it just me, or are you fed up with all this boring French history too?' he hissed at Alexander.

'Well, *I* think it's fascinating. I didn't realise how heavy medieval armour was!' Alexander replied, looking at a picture of a knight in his history book.

'Neither did I – but it doesn't mean I'm interested!' James said, gazing out of the window.

'It's *very* interesting, if you actually *listen*, James! How can you be bored with this? It's great stuff!' Alexander said, folding his arms.

James screwed up a ball of paper and bounced it off his friend's head.

'What was *that* for?' Alexander hissed, rubbing the spot where it had landed.

'Being a goody-goody!' James grinned.

Mr Hall spun round from the whiteboard to find out where the noise was coming from. All he saw was a roomful of pupils, listening hard and looking straight at him.

Funny. I could have sworn I heard whispering . . . he thought to himself. He turned back to the board, where he was preparing a special presentation.

'Today's lesson is about the Battle of Poubelle, in medieval France. I thought it might make our visitors feel at home!' Mr Hall smiled. 'Look carefully at the knights. Their armour is particularly interesting . . .'

'*Told* you!' Alexander whispered.

James stuck out his tongue in response.

As Mr Hall droned on, James slumped down

67

on to his desk, resting his head on his arms.

'Losing . . . will . . . to live!' he groaned at
Lenny, who stifled a giggle.

James stared out of the window once more.
Some year-eights were playing football on the
sports field. Gordon 'The Gorilla' Carver, the
school bully, was thundering up and down the
pitch, barging kids out of the way as he went.

*I wonder if he actually realises he's supposed to follow
the ball?* James thought, idly.

In the staff car park, a flock of seagulls
bickered over the contents of the bins. A delivery
lorry was dropping off great vats of oil and huge
sacks of frozen chips at the kitchens.

*There's Mrs Cooper gossiping with the driver. Bet she
tries to get him inside for a cup of tea . . . yup! There
she goes!* James thought. Mr Wharpley struggled
past with a trolley full of cleaning supplies.

*There's Ms Legg, jogging round the field, and the
year-nines working in the school garden. And there's a*

knight in armour, holding some hag's hand – WHAT?!

James sat bolt upright in his chair. He rubbed his eyes. The knight and the hag were still there, standing by Mr Tick's car.

'James Simpson! Are you listening to me at *all*?' Mr Hall shouted across the classroom.

James spun round to look at the teacher. On the board there was a painting of a medieval knight – and he looked just like the one in the car park!

'S-sorry, sir . . .' he mumbled, sheepishly.

As the teacher turned away, sighing, James's eyes strayed towards the window again. The sun gleamed on the knight's armour.

'This can only mean one thing . . .' he muttered to himself. He nudged Zac, and pointed out of the window.

When Zac saw the knight, he leapt out of his seat. James gently pushed him back down, pointing at Mr Hall. He lifted his finger on to his lips to tell Zac to be quiet.

The boys watched together as the knight and the hag wandered around the sports field, hand in hand. The knight plucked a flower from the prize beds outside the headmaster's study and offered it to the hag with a courtly bow. She seemed to giggle, and tucked the flower into her fuzzy red hair.

'Ewww – I feel a bit sick now . . .' James whispered to Zac.

The French boy stared out of the window, his face pale. He silently shredded a paper tissue as he watched the ghosts through the glass.

As class finished, James grabbed Alexander and Lenny.

'Zac and I need to show you something . . . Look!' He pointed out of the window and the boys saw the two ghosts sitting under a tree.

'What the −! Who's *that*?' Lenny gasped.

Alexander moaned. 'Unless I'm mistaken, that's one of our ghosts − with one of yours!' He pointed out the knight to Isabelle. 'His armour perfectly matches that worn by the knights Mr Hall showed us. I think he's a knight from the time of the Battle of Poubelle!'

Isabelle nodded sadly. '*Oui*, Alexandre. It is so.'

Zac was moving from foot to foot. His eyes were wide.

'It is true! This knight, he haunts L'Ecole de St Martin! He is a terror! He must have − how you say? − *followed* us here from Poubelle!' He shuddered.

'What is it, Zac?' asked James.

Zac looked back at him, his face bleak. 'He won't be alone . . .'

CHAPTER 9
BATTLE PRATTLE

'So, we must rally the troops for a full-scale attack on the school. This is *war*!' Maurice roared.

Edith sighed happily. 'My hero!' she breathed.

'And for a war, we need an army!' Maurice cried, striding around the amphitheatre self-importantly.

'Are you with me, boys?' he shouted to a group of ghosts playing knucklebones in the corner. They looked at each other, then at Maurice. Somebody threw a die. Maurice brandished his sword.

'There is no time for games!' he bellowed, smashing it down between the players. The knucklebones were reduced to powder, and the ghosts scattered.

'Oh, Maurice, you are so powerful and strong!' Edith giggled. 'And so determined! Like a zombie who has spotted a juicy brain!'

Maurice grabbed the ghosts as they tried to slip away.

'Come along, my fine boys! We shall build an army to be proud of!' He marched around the amphitheatre gathering the ghosts together.

Edith rushed after him, poking ghosts and pushing them after Maurice.

'Come along, you lazy lot! Get a move on!' she squawked.

Once they were all assembled, she began barking instructions.

'We need to work together as a fighting machine if we are to rid the school of these noisy, smelly pupils! You must listen to Maurice and do exactly as he says. Maurice?'

The knight rose to his feet. 'To win a war we must train together. We have many wonderful weapons. We have been building a collection of sludge catapults . . .' The knight held up a huge catapult and fired a stinking gobbet of sewer slime at the back wall. It landed with a wet 'splat', showering a passing rat. The sludge slithered down its back, giving it a slimy overcoat.

Edith clapped her hands. '*Wonderful!* That'll have them on the run!' she gushed.

'I have instructed my loyal followers to sharpen bones so there are lethal weapons for us all!' Maurice cried, picking up a wickedly sharp bone and whipping it through the air. It gleamed in the candlelight.

Ambrose frowned. 'Good grief! He's worse than Edith!' he muttered to William.

'I don't want to fight the children, Ambrose –

they're my friends!' the young ghost protested.

Ambrose patted the boy's arm. 'Don't worry,
son – we'll think of a way to scupper their plan!'
he whispered.

William tried to smile. 'I can't risk my friends getting hurt. I'm going to go up top and warn them before Maurice and his barmy army get there,' he declared, sneaking towards the pipes leading up to the school.

'You be careful, lad,' urged Ambrose. 'Meanwhile, I'll see what I can do at this end.' He reached for his leech tin – this called for a snack.

William drifted out of a drain cover in the playground to find James, Lenny and Alexander huddled together with their pen pals, discussing ways to get rid of the ghosts. He listened in.

'Well, we could get one of those TV-show "ghost-buster" crews in to catch them . . .' Lenny said, scratching his head.

'Or, we could lay some sort of trap . . .' James offered.

Alexander's brow furrowed as he thought hard. 'I'm just going to nip to the loo – it often helps me concentrate!'

James hooted with laughter as Alexander wandered off to the toilet block. William quickly seized his chance and concentrated on solidifying. He closed his eyes and pictured Alexander. As that mental picture became clearer, William began to look exactly like the schoolboy. He checked his reflection as he passed a puddle on his way over to the group.

'You're back then! Feeling better?' Lenny laughed.

'Erm . . . yes!' William faltered. Talking to the living always made him a little nervous.

'I've had a great idea! On Friday we can hold a re-enactment of the Battle of Poubelle! The ghosts will hear all the noise and come up out of the sewers to see what they're missing. Then we can bash them!'

'This is a good plan, *non*?' said Zac, nodding to the others.

'It's a great plan!' James grinned.

'And you thought of that on the loo?' Lenny tittered. 'I'll have to go more often!'

'Hey, Alexander – does that mean your brain's in your bum?' James managed to gasp, before he and the others collapsed into a fit of giggles.

'Erm, I've just got to go to my . . . er . . . locker to get my science book,' William stuttered.

'Shall I come with you, Alexandre?' Isabelle asked, wiping the tears of laughter from her eyes and reaching to pick up her bag.

'*No*! I mean . . . er, no, thanks. I'll be back very soon,' said the ghost, and rushed off.

Moments later, the real Alexander came back.

'Sorry I was so long, guys. I got . . .' But nobody was listening. They were all busy discussing some plan to beat the ghosts.

Oh. They've come up with an idea without me,

he thought to himself, feeling a little disappointed.

'Sounds like a winning plan!' he said, squeezing his way back into the huddle.

James gave him an odd look. 'OK, clever clogs, no need to boast!' Alexander was puzzled.

James turned to the others. 'Don't mind the professor here – I think it's the pressure of his enormous brain on his skull, sends him a bit loopy sometimes! Anyway, it's all decided then. We'll get Mr Hall to agree to the re-enactment of the Battle of Poubelle on Friday, but he'll never guess it's a *real* battle we're fighting! That'll teach the French ghosts to mess with St Sebastian's!'

The friends cheered and high-fived each other, then jumped up to go and find the history teacher. Alexander trailed behind them, still baffled.

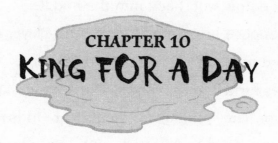

CHAPTER 10
KING FOR A DAY

'Right! Let's find Mr Hall and get this thing organised!' said James as he marched into school. Zac was at his side, and everybody else fell in behind them.

'Oh, look – it's the dweeb mafia!' The Gorilla sneered as they passed.

'Ignore him, Isabelle,' Alexander whispered.

Isabelle scowled at Gordon, then put her nose in the air.

The group of friends stopped outside the staffroom. James nudged Alexander forwards.

'You knock. It was your idea after all,' he hissed.

Alexander grumbled, but knocked reluctantly. Mr Hall came to the door.

'Our luck's in!' Lenny whispered to Manu, who grinned.

'Mr Hall – we were wondering if we could do something really special on Friday to give our visitors a great send off?' Alexander said, in his best 'teacher's pet' voice.

'What did you have in mind, Alexander?' Mr Hall asked, coming out into the corridor and taking a slurp from his mug of coffee.

'Well, we were so inspired by your lesson about the Battle of Poubelle that we had an idea. Could we stage a historically accurate re-enactment of it? We could make props in technology class – it would be amazing!'

Mr Hall gulped down the last of his coffee and placed the mug down on the window sill with a flourish.

'What a *splendid* idea!' he exclaimed, rubbing his hands together. 'It will really bring history to life – and medieval history at that. My greatest love! The Battle of Poubelle, here at St Sebastian's – just imagine! The clash of swords, the battle cries, the moans of the wounded . . . OK – maybe not the last one!' he chuckled. 'Alexander, I always knew you were bright, but you have excelled yourself this time. This exercise will make history the most popular subject in school – just as it should be!'

Mr Hall took a notebook out of his jacket pocket and started making notes. He was so engrossed that he didn't realise the friends were still standing there when he looked up from his scribbling a couple of minutes later.

'Oh! Right! Leave it with me, everyone. I shall consult Mr Tick immediately and then I shall have lots of plans to make. Excellent. Very good. OK – see you all later!' He bounded off along the corridor towards the headmaster's office.

'Well, I'd call that a success!' James laughed, patting Alexander on the shoulder. 'Looks like we'll be battling with some ghosts, come Friday!' he grinned.

'Like that's something to look forward to,' Lenny muttered.

'Well, it's a tough job, but someone's got to do it,' said James.

'Yeah, OK – but does that someone always have to be us?' Lenny moaned.

Meanwhile, Mr Hall burst into Miss Keys's office.

'Is Mr Tick in?' he blurted out.

Miss Keys looked up from the document she was typing at the headmaster's request. It was a press release about the school's French visitors – a sure-fire way to raise his profile among the Grimesford townsfolk.

'Well, he is in, but he said he didn't want to be disturbed. He's very busy today . . .' Miss Keys cautioned. But before she could finish, Mr Hall had bustled enthusiastically into the headmaster's office.

Mr Tick was engrossed in a particularly challenging game of solitaire. He looked up in amazement as Mr Hall burst in, his eyes bright with excitement.

'Mr Tick! Some of the the year-sevens – Alexander in particular –'

Mr Tick held up his hand.

'Let me stop you there, Mr Hall. If Alexander is in any trouble, he will be punished. There are no favourites here at St Sebastian's, and he is well aware of that. Between the hours of nine in the morning and three-twenty in the afternoon, I am Alexander's headmaster, not his beloved father.' Mr Hall looked confused. Mr Tick continued. 'But if my son *is* in any trouble,

I assure you it will have been instigated by that troublesome boy, James Simp—'

'No! No trouble!' Mr Hall smiled. 'Alexander has had the most brilliant idea!'

Mr Tick looked shocked, then he beamed as Mr Hall's words sank in.

'Of course, you know that the apple never falls far from the tree.' The headmaster stroked his lapels proudly.

'Oh, no, headmaster!' said Mr Hall. 'I'm not talking about gravity . . .'

Mr Tick frowned.

For supposedly educated people, teachers can be a dense lot, he thought to himself with a sigh.

'Never mind,' he said, shaking his head. 'Just tell me about the great idea. Let's ignore for just a moment your rude interruption to my, ahem, work . . .' He clicked on his mouse to hide the solitaire game. His 'St Sebastian's – A First Class Education' screensaver slid into place. 'What's so important that you had to rush in here to tell me about it immediately? You know my door is always open for staff issues, but Miss Keys is the gatekeeper. I'm a busy man – a very busy man.'

'Yes, M-M-Mr Tick – of course! I just got carried away by m-m-my enthusiasm,' Mr Hall stammered. Being in Mr Tick's office always made him a little nervous.

'For goodness' sake, man – spit it out! What did you want to tell me about?' growled Mr Tick, taking a sip of his coffee from his prized 'Solitaire Champ' mug.

Mr Hall's face was bright pink.

'An idea!' Mr Hall was smiling again. 'A battle!'

'A *what*?' Mr Tick spluttered.

'A battle, Mr Tick,' beamed the history teacher.

'Oh, yes, a battle. Of course. Why didn't I think of that? Who needs an education when they can just have a jolly good fight?' he said, sarcastically. 'Are you out of your *mind*? Have you taken leave of your *senses*? I think the school governors would rather see the pupils take a more *appropriate* approach to problem-solving than *full-scale battle*, Mr Hall.'

'Oh, no! I didn't mean . . . what I meant was a *pretend* battle,' Mr Hall struggled to explain.

'To solve non-existent problems, I suppose?' Mr Tick sneered.

'No! No! A re-enactment *here*, at St Sebastian's! Like they sometimes have at historic buildings. You know – you take a picnic and watch the Vikings invade, or a Battle of Britain dogfight . . .' Mr Hall explained.

'Yes, yes – I know exactly what you mean. Actually, that's a good idea. A very good idea.' Mr Tick rubbed his chin, and Mr Hall sighed with relief.

This is harder to explain than I expected! he thought.

'Yes,' Mr Tick continued, 'this could be a superb opportunity for some publicity for me – I mean,

St Sebastian's! It will be a great way to make our French visitors feel valued. It will let them know how much we have enjoyed their visit, and how much effort we have put in to it. We will be bound to be invited back to Poubelle for a visit.' He grinned, wolfishly.

All that cheap French champagne . . . I wonder how many crates would fit in the boot of the school bus? It's not as though the children need room for cases . . . he thought to himself.

'We'll do it!' he smiled. He flipped through his leather-bound desk diary, running through appointments under his breath. 'Solitaire . . . lunch at The Copper Kettle . . . an appointment at the golf club . . .'

'Erm, Mr Tick? The pupils suggested Friday, if that's OK with you. I know you're a busy man . . .' Mr Hall burbled.

Mr Tick frowned at the interruption.

'Yes. Friday, at two,' said the headmaster,

taking control of the arrangements. 'That will give me time for a nice long lun– *meeting* first.' He cleared his throat noisily. 'Now – you hurry along and get things orgnanised, Mr Hall.'

Mr Tick buzzed the intercom to call Miss Keys. 'I have an exciting addition to that press release, Miss Keys. Please come in straight away.'

Mr Hall seized the chance to dash off, muttering, 'Baking foil for armour, wood for swords . . .'

The next morning, in assembly, Mr Tick shared the news with the rest of the school.

'Good morning. *Bonjour!*' He simpered from the stage. 'I have excellent news! Friday afternoon, we go into battle!'

The hall was filled with murmuring. People looked at each other in confusion.

'Just my little joke!' Mr Tick continued. 'We are going to round off the wonderful visit from our French friends with a historical spectacular! A special treat – the re-enactment of a glorious moment from their past – the Battle of Poubelle! Mr Hall will now explain the details. Mr Hall?'

Mr Tick smiled at the history teacher and gestured to the front of the stage before taking his seat.

'Ehem . . . yes!' Mr Hall began, nervously gazing out at the sea of pupils. 'Year-seven pupils will be divided into two camps under the leadership of the French king, Phillipe the Second, and the German emperor, Otto the Fourth. I shall also be asking some carefully selected older pupils to be responsible for their safety at all times.'

'Yes – pupil safety is of great importance to the staff and the governors . . .' Mr Tick added, hastily.

'The headmaster has decided that the part of the French king should be played by the boy who came up with this wonderful scheme – Alexander Tick!' Mr Hall said, pointing into the crowd. Heads swivelled to stare at the schoolboy, who blushed red to the roots of his hair.

'But I didn't!' he whispered to James.

James frowned, looking puzzled.

'Well, duh! Yes you did! When you were on the lav, remember?' he whispered.

'What?' It was Alexander's turn to look puzzled.

'And the part of the German emperor, Otto the Fourth will be played by . . .' A hand thrust a piece of paper towards Mr Hall. He read out the name scrawled on it. 'Erm . . . Gordon Carver.'

'He's not technically a year-seven, but it'll give him some responsibility and help him to manage his behaviour!' Ms Byron, the school librarian said, brightly.

And keep him out of my library session this

afternoon, she thought, relieved. She winced as she remembered the time he had destroyed a set of expensive biology books by highlighting all the 'naughty' words in yellow pen.

Gordon punched the air and grimaced. Then he punched the boy next to him hard enough to give him a dead arm.

'Ow! What was *that* for?' the boy moaned.

'Because I am the emperor – and you are my serf!' Gordon crowed.

Great. I can see this ending badly, thought Mr Hall. He managed to smile bravely. 'Ah, yes. Anyway. Um . . . I'll be issuing armour and weapons after lunch. In the meantime, please look to your leaders for instructions. I shall give them details of the original battle strategies after this assembly. Have fun!'

As the pupils left the hall, the history teacher handed Alexander a stack of papers about the battle. His friends mobbed him as soon as they were safe from Mr Tick's beady eyes.

'Hey – your majesty! Are you still going to talk to us mere peasants?' James called, clapping Alexander on the back. 'Oops! Perhaps I shouldn't be touching the royal person!' he laughed, theatrically removing his hands from Alexander's back and holding them up in surrender. Alexander blushed again.

'Come along now!' said Mr Hall, ushering them towards his classroom. 'It's time for another history lesson! There'll be plenty of time to pay homage to your king later!'

By break time, Alexander was becoming royally sick of his friends' jibes.

'I prefer to be the one telling the jokes myself,' he said with a sigh.

'Actually, I thought Leandra's was quite funny,' Lenny smiled.

'I suppose so . . .' Alexander sighed. 'But when she said, "What's the first thing a king or queen does when they come to the throne?" I thought she was asking me a serious question. Then, when I started giving her answers, she just smacked me on the back of the head and said, "Duh – no!

They *sit* down." I felt like a right fool!' he said, slapping his forehead with his hand. 'Never mind! We've got the battle to think about now, anyway,' James said, punching Alexander gently on the arm. 'Cheer up!'

The friends all spent the rest of break practising fighting formations and battle strategy. Alexander's face shone with excitement.

'Oh, how I love history!' he sighed, contentedly. 'James, Lenny – you'll need to be faster on that counter-attack. Isabelle, Zac – run up the side there and make sure we're protected. Manu – cover my back.'

As the king barked instructions, his army grumbled and huffed.

'I suppose it'll all be worth it in the end,' James muttered through gritted teeth. 'Anything to get rid of those ghosts.'

'It had better be!' Lenny groaned, trudging off on yet another 'royal' errand.

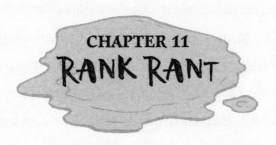

CHAPTER 11
RANK RANT

A crimson sun peeped over the horizon of
St Sebastian's playing field.

'It is a glorious day for battle!' Count Maurice
roared, swishing his sword about in the air
dramatically. 'Look at the omen in the sky!
These battlefields shall run red with the blood
of our foes!' Edith sighed happily.

William shuddered. 'That's my friends he's
talking about!' he despaired.

'Don't worry, young William. Look around
you. Can you see a bloodthirsty army anywhere

around here?' Ambrose soothed.

William looked around him at the plague-pit ghosts practising their combat skills. Two young spirits were making up a dance that involved jumping over their swords. Every time they made a mistake they collapsed in a giggling heap.

Behind Edith, Bertram Ruttle was conducting the Plague Pit Junior Ghost Band with a thighbone. They were supposed to be rehearsing their battle march, but they were picking out a calypso instead. The tall ghost grinned happily and wiggled his bottom.

'Hey, William!' he called. 'Move your feet to the beat!'

As William wandered across the field, he heard groups of ghosts complaining about Maurice and his friends.

'I don't know who he thinks he is – barging in here, throwing his ectoplasm around! He can't tell us what to do!' one phantom complained.

'I know! I always thought Edith was a miserable old mare, but she's nothing compared to that pompous man!' a haughty lady ghost said, pursing her lips. 'Personally, I intend to do a thoroughly bad job. I couldn't face eternity under his rule. I'd have to find a little cottage to haunt somewhere. It just isn't on!'

William walked on. Ambrose joined him.

'I've just been listening to that huddle of ghosts over there,' the older ghost said. 'They're discussing strategies all right, but not battle strategies – ideas for scuppering Maurice's plans!'

William smiled.

'This is *great*! If we all pull together and do a terrible job, Maurice might finally realise he's wasting his time and that we don't want him here!' William beamed.

'Absolutely,' agreed Ambrose. 'I never thought I'd say this, but I miss the old days before Maurice and his miserable mob arrived, back when Edith was in charge. I know she's a rotten old crow, but better the rotten old crow we know, I say. At least, we know how to deal with her. This Maurice is a pain in the ectoplasm – always marching about, declaring orders. I'm sick of it!'

'And that armour of his sounds like a cutlery drawer being thrown down the stairs when he walks about. It brings on my headaches!' Lady Grimes moaned, lifting a delicate hand to her forehead.

Ambrose hugged her sympathetically.

By this time, the first pupils were being dropped off at school by their parents. The sound of car doors slamming drowned out the noise of combat practice – what there was of it.

'Everybody! Below!' Maurice ordered.

'There he goes again,' grumbled Ambrose. 'That's *it*! He'll have to go!' he sighed, as they drifted back towards the sewer. 'Mind you, I

don't think we have much to worry about, my
love,' he said, taking Lady Grimes's hand.

'Ambrose! Stop teasing and give that back!'
Lady Grimes giggled. She snatched her hand
back playfully and tucked it into her velvet
sleeve. 'Why shouldn't we worry?'

'We saw the pupils practising their own mock battle here yesterday. They were brilliant! I'll tell you now, the sight of that lot charging towards me would make me turn tail and run! They were wailing like banshees and swinging their weapons fit to see off any army Maurice can muster! Those French ghosts will soon be running for home, you mark my words. They'll be on that coach back to France quicker than you can say "Battle of Poubelle!"' He roared with laughter.

Edith heard him and scowled ferociously. She went to bellow at Ambrose, but Maurice caught her hand and kissed it.

'Come, my sweet. We must prepare for the glorious battle of St Sebastian's. I shall be fighting for your colours, *non*?' Edith sighed happily.

'Yeah – but does he know her colours are bogey green and pus yellow? Very pretty ...' Ambrose chuckled.

'Pretty awful!' William agreed, laughing.

CHAPTER 12
A FIGHTING CHANCE

At 2 p.m., a special bell rang in school.

'Let battle commence!' Mr Tick boomed.

A rumbling sound filled the air.

Below, in the amphitheatre, chunks of cement brickwork rained down on to the assembled ghosts.

'What's that noise?' Edith asked, looking up.

A large spider fell on to her face. It flinched at

the stench of Edith's breath and scuttled away.

'I confess I am baffled,' Maurice said, shaking his head. 'It sounds like a *grande* army galloping into battle. A wondrous and inspiring noise, *oui*?'

'I'd wee too if I was him,' William whispered to Ambrose. 'He's really got it coming to him.'

'No, William, he said *oui*, not "wee",' Lady Grimes explained. 'It means "yes" in French.'

'Cor! Those French folks are a bit rude! If my mum had asked me if I'd fed the chickens and I'd said "wee" she would have clouted me one!' said William.

'No, William. "Yes" – not "wee",' Lady Grimes smiled, kindly.

'Sorry, you've lost me . . .' puzzled William.

'Never mind, my dear. Let's just leave it, shall we?' said Lady Grimes, patiently. 'I think we'd better concentrate on finding out what that strange noise is. I do hope the sewer's not crumbling or we'll be homeless!'

'I recognise that noise. It's not the sewer, it's the children!' said Ambrose. 'The last time I heard a stampede like that, there was a rumour that the tuck shop were giving out free sweets! They must be preparing for the battle!'

'It is time, my brave comrades!' Maurice barked, bashing his sword on his huge shield to get everyone's attention. 'May every ghost here fight until their last breath!'

'I don't know about you, but my last breath was about six hundred years ago,' Ambrose whispered to Lady Grimes. She tittered.

'We must uphold the honour of my rotting lady fair, Edith Codd!' Edith's eyes shone. Maurice continued with his speech. 'Let us fight with hearts of lions and arms of bears!'

'We're going to look a bit daft like that . . .' Ambrose chuckled quietly.

When William glanced round, he saw that his friend had morphed into a strange creature with a huge, shaggy mane and paws that ended in wicked claws.

'Careful, Ambrose – he'll see you!' William hissed, elbowing him.

Ambrose changed back, grinning sheepishly.

'I shall charge into battle with your name upon my cold, dead lips!' Maurice declared to Edith.

'Better that than having *her* on his lips – yuck!' Ambrose chuckled.

Edith glared at him.

'To the pipes!' Maurice cried.

The plague-pit ghosts trailed after him half-heartedly.

'He's too full of himself to notice that nobody's interested in fighting apart from him and his cronies,' grumbled William.

'And his lady love,' Ambrose added. 'Still, their eyes will soon be opened when they get up top.'

As the ghosts drifted out of pipes and drains, they looked around at the empty school.

'These cowards, they have heard of my battle skills and have run away, *non*?' Maurice said, puffing his chest out proudly.

'That would be a definite *non*, I think,' Ambrose said, pointing out of the window. Hundreds of pupils were swarming across the sports field brandishing swords, battleaxes and spears. Maurice's eyes widened.

'How can they have heard our battle plans? I do not believe it . . .' he murmured, his shoulders sagging.

'Well, even if they've heard from a *spy*,' Edith glared at William, who suddenly found his feet incredibly interesting, 'there's no turning back now! We've sworn to rid St Sebastian's of these pesky children – and that's just what we'll do!'

She charged off into the playground, pushing pupils aside as she passed. As she plunged deeper

into the crowd, she called back to rally the troops.

'Come on! We can do this! You heard Maurice – you're supposed to be upholding my honour! Attaaack!'

Behind her, a motley crew of reluctant plague-pit ghosts stopped chatting and raised their sludge catapults and sharpened bones, attempting to look fierce for her benefit. As soon as she'd raced off, flailing her skinny arms and whirling through the crowd like a demon, they downed arms and picked up where they'd left off.

Several groups of phantoms ambled off to play knuckle bones. The Headless Horseman started a game of kick-about with some of the younger ghosts, using his head for a ball. Bertram gave a signal to the Plague Pit Junior Ghost Band, who struck up a rendition of the musical ghost's self-penned song 'Edith Is A Loony' to the tune of a jaunty rumba. Ambrose tapped his feet.

'Like it?' grinned Bertram. His friend nodded.

'It's a one-off – just like the woman herself,' he laughed, watching the old hag fruitlessly launching sludge missiles at the St Sebastian's pupils. Most of them seemed too busy dodging The Gorilla to really notice her.

'What's that *disgusting* smell?' a small boy exclaimed as Edith ran past him, panting. 'Last time I smelt something that bad, I'd stepped in it!'

Edith frowned at the boy, but battled on regardless. Alexander saw her and slashed at her with his sword.

'The enemy king!' she screeched. 'See his fine armour!'

'Actually, it's tin foil with bubble wrap underneath for texture,' grinned James, joining the action. 'Looks the part though, Your Majesty!' he said to Alexander.

Edith looked behind her for reinforcements.

'Maurice, help me!' she cried. 'Oh.'

Edith watched as her knight in shining armour

beat a hasty retreat. Maurice and his cronies
were creeping around the edge of the staff car
park, towards the main sewer outlet. A bird,
startled by the noise, flew out of a bush and
Maurice shrieked, dropping his sword and shield
with a clatter.

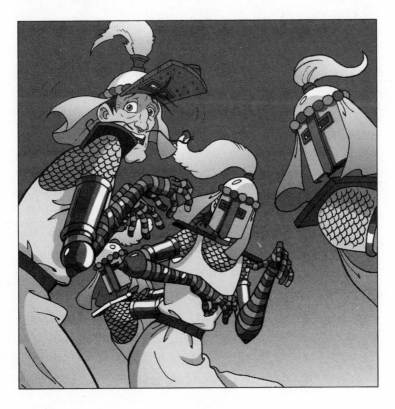

It was loud enough to be heard over the battle, and Ambrose turned to see what was going on, then glanced at Edith.

'From the look on the old hag's face, that's not the only clanger good old Maurice has dropped today!' he laughed.

The French ghosts were not alone in fleeing the battle. A steady stream of plague-pit ghosts was wafting away from the battle.

'See!' Ambrose pointed at the stream of spirits heading for the sewer. 'I told you there was nothing to worry about. Their hearts just weren't in it. And now that wolf in sheep's clothing has been shown up for the coward he really is!' He threw back his head and laughed.

'Where's Edith?' William asked.

'Look – there she is!' shouted Ambrose.

Edith was surrounded by a vicious-looking troupe of girls who were poking her with their swords. She in turn swiped at them with a clawed hand and shrieked terrible oaths at them.

'I suppose we'd better help her . . .' William said, looking concerned.

'Oh, if we must . . .' his friend sighed. They drifted across to the group of girls. 'Look! A famous bard!' Ambrose shouted, pointing towards the school gates.

The girls looked around, baffled.

'A famous bird? Where?' a studious-looking girl asked.

'They call them pop stars now, Ambrose,' William giggled. 'I heard it on Mr Wharpley's radio.'

'Very well. Look! A pop star!' Ambrose bellowed. 'Near the gates!'

The girls sped off, completely forgetting their opponent.

Edith slumped to the floor.

'Ambrose! You came to my rescue . . .' she whimpered.

'I would have thought you'd had enough of knights in shining armour for one day, Edith,' Lady Grimes said firmly, pulling Edith to her feet. 'Come along now. I think it's time to go and give that Maurice a piece of your mind!'

Edith nodded and brushed off her clothes.

'Are you sure she's got any to spare?' Ambrose whispered, earning a sharp look from Lady Grimes.

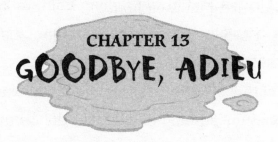

CHAPTER 13
GOODBYE, ADIEU

On the sports field, the pupils battled on. Lenny gave Gordon a sly whack across the back of the legs with the flat of his sword.

'Ow! Who did that?' The Gorilla raged.

Lenny grinned and held his hand out to Alexander for a high five.

'For you, emperor!' he laughed, bowing over-dramatically before the bully. At that moment, a shrill whistle stopped the armies in their tracks.

'Aha! Well-trained troops – that's what I like to see!' Ms Legg smiled. 'It's time for our visitors to get back on their coach, I'm afraid. They have to return to Cricklebrooke to pick up their luggage before the long journey home.'

'I can't believe it's over already!' Alexander moaned. 'I was having a great time!'

'Of course you were, Alexander. We all were,' Mr Tick said, pushing himself into the centre of the children and posing as a photographer from the local paper arrived to take a picture.

'Well, nobody can say it hasn't been an interesting visit!' James laughed, as the year-sevens all said their goodbyes 'It's been great having you here as part of the gang,' he said, high-fiving Zac.

'*Oui*, but your hag, she is terrible, *non*?' Zac shuddered.

'Oh, she's that all right!' laughed Lenny. 'And as for your fella in armour – well, I wouldn't like to meet him on a dark night.'

'Don't you mean a dark *knight*?' Alexander joked.

Isabelle groaned and punched him lightly on the arm.

'I shall miss your jokes, Alexandre! You are *très* . . . very funny!'

'Please come and visit Poubelle,' said Manu. 'We will show you all of the sights!'

'As long as it doesn't include a tour of any knights' tombs!' Lenny laughed, nervously.

'I heard Dad telling Madame Dupont to plan a return trip – although that might just have been for the reporter's benefit – so we may get a chance!' said Alexander, hopefully.

'Well, we got those ghosts on the run anyway!' James smiled. 'You never know, they may be too scared to make another appearance at your school now! Nothing like a bit of teamwork!'

'I hope so, James,' said Zac. 'I will not – how you say? – count my gooses before they get cooked, *non*?' He looked surprised by the gale of laughter that followed his comment.

'Oh, Zac – we're really going to miss you lot!'
James laughed.

At that moment, the clapped-out old coach
that had brought the pen pals to St Sebastian's
chugged back up the school drive. The pupils
swapped promises to write, and they meant it –
even James and Lenny.

'We can email, too!' Alexander shouted, as
their friends boarded the bus. Madame Dupont
beamed.

'I take it the visit was a great success, *non*?' she
asked the pupils standing on the tarmac.

'*Oui, oui, madame!*' Alexander answered.

'Ha! Stick said "wee wee" – to a teacher!'
James whispered. 'Let's tell his dad!'

The boys fell about laughing and waved to
their friends as the coach pulled away on the
first leg of the long journey back to France.

Down in the sewer, things were rather less friendly.

'How *could* you! How COULD you? Desert your posts . . . desert your . . . your . . . oh!' Edith shrieked, exasperated. 'I have never seen such cowardice in the face of an enemy!' She spat on the floor in disgust. A passing rat accidentally stepped in it and zoomed off, squealing. 'Call yourself a knight? A KNIGHT? You are not even a man!' the old hag screamed.

'She's working up a fine head of steam there!' Ambrose chuckled.

'You and your cronies,' she gestured towards the group of French ghosts standing behind Maurice, 'are pathetic specimens! You even manage to make Bertram and Ambrose look useful!'

'Erm, thanks – I suppose,' Ambrose mumbled.

'Why don't you crawl back to where you came from? – I never want to see you *ever again*!' Maurice hung his head in shame. 'And *that* can go, too!' she squawked, kicking the bottom of the bone statue of Maurice that his followers had built in the middle of the amphitheatre. The structure swayed and creaked.

'You have made a mockery of us all and we will not stand for it!' she hissed angrily through her teeth.

At that moment, the statue began to topple. It bent in the middle, then bones began cascading down, skulls skittering all over the cavern floor.

'NOOO!' bellowed Bertram, as he charged towards the tumbling structure. 'Help me!' he called to a group of ghosts nearby.

They caught the bones as they fell, and Bertram soon had them safely bundled into sacks. He scowled at Maurice as he dragged them away. 'No respect for other people's property . . .' he muttered as he went. Maurice sank even lower.

'Right! That's it! *Out!*' Edith yelled. Maurice looked up at her one last time, his eyes full of shame.

123

'But Edith! I would have made you my *lady*. We could have ruled this place together . . .' he whispered in a broken voice.

'*Lady*? *Ruled*? Never! You meant nothing to me. You hear me? NOTHING! Even less than nothing! Get *out*!' Edith roared.

'Well, William my lad, they do say "Hell hath no fury like a woman scorned" and you can double that for Edith! Look at her go!'

By now, the old hag was pushing and shoving the French ghosts towards the sewer outlet.

'Go on! Get away with you! Go back to your own miserable school and leave us in peace!' she shrieked.

'You can't help but be impressed though . . .' Lady Grimes said, quietly. 'There she is, broken-hearted, but she still manages to stamp her own amazing style on the whole proceedings. Marvellous . . .'

'Actually, I think she's just trying to stamp on

Maurice's head!' Ambrose chuckled.

With one last look at Edith, Maurice raised his sword to admit defeat and pointed it towards the sewer outlet. The French ghosts trudged along behind him, looking at the floor.

'Good riddance to bad rubbish!' Edith snorted, rubbing her hands together at a job well done. She slumped down next to her upturned barrel and closed her eyes, sighing heavily.

Lady Grimes patted her hand and her eyes flew open.

'Oh! For a moment there, I thought . . .' Edith said, sadly.

'I know, dear, I know,' Lady Grimes smiled, kindly.

Then Edith spotted a ghost sleeping under a bone bench and the moment was gone.

'You! Move your lazy self and help with the clearing up. There's no room for slackers and shirkers here! Get on with it! This amphitheatre needs sweeping from top to bottom. Bring some fresh sludge in . . . and those cobwebs don't just festoon prettily by themselves, you know.'

'She's back,' William whispered.

'And for once, my young friend, I'm rather glad to see her!' Ambrose said, cracking a lopsided smile.

Up on the surface, it had started to rain. The French ghosts were being lashed by sharp needles of icy water, and the wind kept whipping away clumps of their ectoplasm.

'Well, the sooner we find the coach the better, I suppose,' Maurice mumbled, miserably.

'Erm, my lord?' his man-servant ghost whispered.

'What is it? Speak up, man!' Maurice snapped.

'The coach . . .'

'What about it? Where is it?' Maurice scanned the car park.

'There!' The runty spectre pointed to the hill beyond the school gates. A small, coach-shaped dot was chugging away up the road.

'It's going to be a long walk home, sire.'

'NOOOOOO!' Maurice gave an agonized shriek.

Down in the sewer, Edith heard. She smiled. It wasn't a pretty smile, but it warmed the plague-pit ghosts' spectral hearts all the same.

'Never mind, Edith,' Lady Grimes soothed.

'*Mind*? Why would I *mind*? I was only putting up with that tin man to see if he could help us in our battle against St Sebastian's!' Edith sniffed. 'This is *my* sewer, and no slimy knight in shining armour is going to take it away from me!'

Edith kicked the last pieces of Maurice's statue around the floor in a furious frenzy, stomping on the plaque that read 'Count Maurice' for good measure.

'Good riddance to bad rubbish, I say!' she growled, grinding a piece of the statue into sewer sludge with her foot. 'I'm in charge here and no one should forget it!' She stared around the amphitheatre, as though daring anyone to argue with her.

'One day soon, all of St Sebastian's will be mine – *mine*, I say!' she cackled, her eyes glowing red in the gloom.

SURNAME: Dupont

FIRST NAME: Sylvie

AGE: 45

HEIGHT: 1.6 metres

EYES: Brown

HAIR: Dark brown

FACT FILE

LIKES: Cookery - Madame Dupont can rustle up a wide range of tasty French recipes when she's not teaching French

DISLIKES: The horrible English food they serve in the school canteen

SPECIAL SKILL: Can wrap Mr Tick round her little finger by fluttering her eyelashes at him and speaking in her French accent

INTERESTING FACT: Madame Dupont secretly wanted to be a chef, but abandoned her cookery studies to become a French teacher, although she still longs for the great food of her home country

For more facts on Sylvie Dupont, go to www.too-ghoul.com

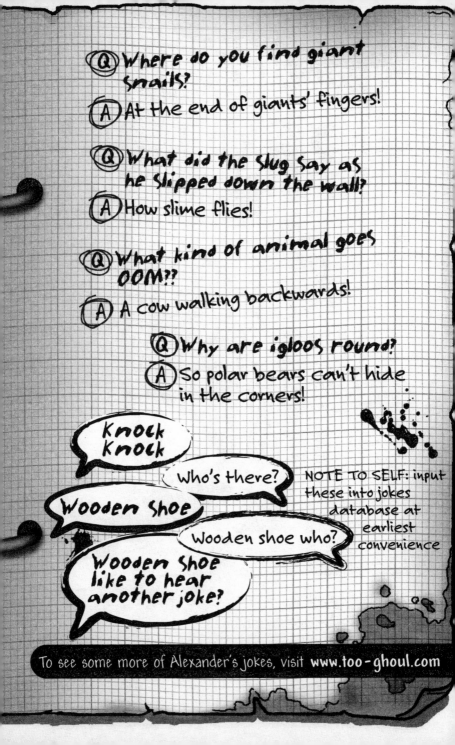

What Zey Eet in England

Zees ees some mistake. Zees are rock hard, like zee bullets

Smells like le sewage – do not eat!

I theenk zees is food, but eet has no taste. Could be used for beelding houses?

Ghost Army Tactics
Sewer weaponry and how to use it

Slime catapault
Fill pouch with raw sewage, aim, and fire. Use of goggles recommended, as can backfire with nasty consequences.

Leech-shooter
Fire little blood-sucking monsters at your enemy. Careful they don't escape from your trouser pocket — or get eaten by Ambrose first!

Bone spear
Leg bones work best. Make sure you remove feet first. Sharpen one end, lob at pesky schoolchildren.

Toilet water
Scooped from the bowl of a haunted toilet. Known to peel wallpaper and make eyes water at a hundred paces. Cover nose when using.

Rib boomerang
These take a bit of skill to throw. Make sure they don't knock your head off when they come back around!

Coffin-lid shield
Use to deflect enemy attacks and to shield eyes form fearsomely ugly ghosts. Can be used as a surfboard after battle.

Can't wait for the next book in the series?
Here's a sneak preview of

TEAM SPIRIT

available now from all good bookshops,
or **www.too-ghoul.com**

CHAPTER 1
SAFE HANDS

'OOOOF!'

Alexander Tick winced as the football crunched into his stomach.

'Rubbish! You could have caught that one!' yelled his friend, James Simpson, from across the street. 'Sorry, did that hurt, mate?'

Alexander was writhing around on the ground, gasping for breath.

'No, you idiot!' he wheezed, pulling himself to his feet. 'I was practising my break-dancing. Of *course* it hurt!'

James shrugged. 'Well, maybe you should try actually *catching* the ball this time?' he suggested, taking another shot at Alexander.

'OOOOOOARGH!'

Alexander lunged at the ball, but it slapped him hard in the face and he went flying across the pavement. James sighed, and watched silently as his friend climbed out of a prickly-looking hedge.

'I nearly got that one, didn't I?' Alexander whimpered, pulling a leaf out of his hair.

'No, Stick,' sighed James. 'You nearly destroyed that garden. Now come here and let me give you a secret goalkeeping tip.'

Alexander crossed the street, rearranging his blazer. 'A secret tip? Where'd you hear it?' he asked.

'From a professional goalie I met,' James said, putting his arm round the friend's shoulders. 'You sure you're ready for it?'

Alexander nodded. 'I need all the advice I can get – the year-seven cup final's only two days off!'

James leant in close to Alexander and lowered his voice. 'Right. Here's the secret. It'll really help.'

Alexander nodded again.

'It's a sure-fire way to improve your skills,' James whispered, deadly serious.

Alexander nodded and held his breath.

'KEEP YOUR EYES *OPEN*, YOU IDIOT!'
James bellowed at the top of his voice in
Alexander's ear.

'AAAAAAAAAAAAAARGH!' Alexander
cried, almost jumping out of his skin.

James doubled over laughing, clutching his sides.
He was still giggling when the third member of
their gang, Lenny Maxwell, rounded the corner
of the street.

'What's going on, you two?' Lenny said,
lumbering up to them with his hands in his
pockets. 'Why've you got leaves in your hair,
Alexander?'

James wiped the tears from his eyes and
slapped Lenny on the back.

'Just giving Alexander some training for the
cup final!' he snorted, struggling to get his
laughter under control. 'But he's still scared of
the ball! Maybe you can talk some sense into
him Lenny . . .'

Lenny raised his eyebrows and looked down at Alexander.

'You know, Stick, the ball's the least of your worries. It's our opponents you should be panicking about. St Mary's are a real bunch of leg-breakers!' Lenny said, reassuringly.

James stared at Lenny in mock surprise. 'Good one, Lenny!' he said, sarcastically. 'That'll really build up his confidence!'

'Well, it's true!' cried Lenny. 'They're terrifying! The smallest member of their team is bigger than me, and they got banned from the cup last year for sticking a corner flag up the referee's . . . OWWWW! What was *that* for?'

James had given Lenny a sharp kick to the shin.

'To shut you up!' said James, nodding at Alexander, who was shaking like a leaf. 'Look at him!'

'Well, St Mary's must be pretty tough!' Lenny said to James as they walked. 'We're only in the cup final cos no other school would play them!'

Alexander moped along a few paces behind
the other two.

'Why, oh, *why* do I have to play in goal?' he
wailed. 'I'm virtually allergic to any sort of sport!
Last summer I had to have a week off school after
a particularly energetic game of chess, remember?'

James ruffled Alexander's hair.

'You know why you're in the team, Stick!' he
said. 'Cos Ben "Safe Hands" Fletcher broke his
finger last week, and you're our reserve!'

Lenny shuddered. 'Yeah, that was nasty.
Picking his nose when the school bus crashed . . .
Imagine the pain!' he muttered, rubbing his own
nose for comfort.

Alexander scowled at them both. 'I'm only
substitute goalie cos my dad's the headmaster!'
he complained. 'He *made* me sign up! I never
thought I'd actually have to *play*! I *hate* football!'

James began juggling the ball on his knee as he

walked along. 'You hate all sorts of stuff, Stick,' he said, flicking the ball over a passing paper boy. 'Music, sport, games, weekends, holidays, fun . . .'

'Oh, shut up!' grumbled Alexander. 'I just enjoy the more intellectual things in life, that's all – like chemistry, biology and physics. I'll have you know, I had a great weekend studying the effects of sodium on . . . OOOF!'

The ball hit Alexander right in the chest, taking his breath away and making him drop his schoolbag.

'How about studying the effects of a football on the human body, Stick?' James laughed.

'I'll study the effects of my foot on your backside in a minute!' gasped Alexander, giving James a dead arm.

'Aaaaargh!' James wailed. 'How does someone as weedy as you give such bad dead arms, Stick?'

Alexander smirked to himself. 'Cos I studied the muscles of the upper arm in my biology textbook last night!' he smiled.

'Knock it off, you two!' Lenny shouted. 'This is important! We've got to play a team that beat us thirty-seven–nil last year in just two days' time. Could we please focus on our football practice?'

James just dribbled round Lenny and ran off down the street. 'Practice? I don't need practice!' he yelled over his shoulder. 'I'm the super-striker that's gonna save the day! Hat-trick here I come!'

Lenny and Alexander watched him disappear off up the street. Lenny looked down at his shorter friend.

'Come on!' he said, trying to cheer him up. 'How about telling me one of your famous jokes?'

Alexander smiled. He loved jokes almost as much as he hated sport.

'Well, if you will twist my arm . . . Why do babies make great footballers?' he grinned.

Lenny shrugged his shoulders.

'Cos they're always dribbling!' Alexander cried.

Lenny rolled his eyes.

'I don't care how nasty St Mary's are, Stick,' he complained as they reached the school gates, 'playing them can't be any worse than listening to your gags!'

Mr Tick stood at the school gates with his hands on his hips.

'Come along!' he bellowed down the street at the hordes of reluctant pupils trudging into school.

He watched as his son and two other boys larked about all the way down the grimy old street that led to St Sebastian's.

'Alexander! That means you, too!' he shouted.

Mr Tick was not in a good mood. He liked to get at least three games of solitaire in before the school day started, but the school secretary, Miss Keys, had interrupted him twice that morning and he hadn't finished a single one.

He frowned as he saw James run through the gates with his school jumper over his head. *Why can't Alexander be a bit more sporty?* he thought to himself. *Oh, well. I'm sure a spell in the school football team will toughen him up!*

'Hurry up, you boys,' he roared, 'or you'll be in detention all week!'

Mr Tick checked his tie in a car mirror, smoothed his hair down and inspected his teeth.

'Looking smart, headmaster,' he told his reflection. 'Very sharp indeed!'

He was so busy preening himself that he didn't notice a thick blob of stinking, gooey slime appear from thin air and land with a dollop on one of his Italian leather shoes.

He didn't even notice as it oozed round his shoe, giving off a foul, deadly stench. He was far too busy striding importantly back to his office. If he hurried, he might get a game of solitaire in before assembly started.